D0390977

Special thanks to Venetia Davie, Ryan Ferguson, Charnita Belcher, Tanya Mann, Julia Phelps, Sharon Woloszyk, Nicole Corse, Darren Sander, Rita Lichtwardt, Carla Alford, Julia Pistor, Renata Marchand, Michelle Cogan, ARC Productions and Michael Goguen

Published in the United States by Random House Children's Books, a division of Penguin Random House LLC, 1745 Broadway, New York, NY 10019, and in Canada by Random House of Canada, a division of Penguin Random House Ltd., Toronto.
Random House and the colophon are registered trademarks of Penguin Random House LLC.

ISBN 978-0-553-53764-2 (trade) — ISBN 978-0-553-53765-9 (ebook)
randomhousekids.com
Printed in the United States of America 10 9 8 7 6 5 4 3 2 1 First Edition

Adapted by Devin Ann Wooster

Based on the screenplay by Amy Wolfram

Illustrated by Lora Lee

Random House 🏠 New York

It was a warm summer afternoon in the little town of Willows, Wisconsin. A gentle wind blew through the town's famous willow trees.

Barbie drove a pink camper. Skipper, Stacie, and Chelsea rode with her. They were starting their summer vacation. They were going to stay in Willows for two weeks!

"Are we there yet?" Chelsea asked. She was the youngest of the sisters and didn't remember Willows.

Barbie remembered Willows well. It was her hometown. Her grandmother still lived there. Barbie couldn't wait to spend time with Grandma Roberts again. She also wanted to go to Willowfest with her friend Christie.

Barbie drove into the center of town. They passed the town's first willow tree. It had grown from a twig planted by the town's founders. All the other willow trees in town came from that first tree.

Barbie saw the ice cream shop. "I was Junior Scooper of the Month nine months in a row!" Barbie said.

The girls also saw the clock tower and city hall. Two men, Joe and Marty, were putting up a tent for Willowfest.

Barbie turned down a tree-lined road. The girls saw a pretty house. Grandma Roberts stood on the porch.

The girls jumped out of the camper. "Grandma!" they shouted.

"You've all gotten so big!" Grandma said. She hugged them. "Girls, I have a surprise for you."

"I love, love, love surprises!" Chelsea

said. She raced into the house. Where was the surprise?

Chelsea and Stacie went into the kitchen.

"Cupcakes!" Chelsea said. Grandma had baked cupcakes. Yummy!

"Look under the cupcakes." Grandma smiled.

Was there another surprise?

Chelsea looked under the cupcakes. She looked under the plate. Then she looked under the table. She found Grandma's dog, Tiffany—and something else!

"Puppies!" Chelsea squealed. "Oh, they're so cute!"

There were four tiny puppies in a basket. They were excited, too. The puppies started talking to each other. But Barbie, Skipper, Stacie, and Chelsea only heard their puppy barks.

"Mama," one puppy said, "those girls are so cute!"

The puppy jumped onto Chelsea and licked her face. Chelsea giggled.

"I'm going to call you Honey!" Chelsea said.

Honey turned to Tiffany. "Can I keep her?" she asked.

A spotted brown puppy tumbled out of the basket. She climbed all the way up Stacie's leg! Stacie named her Rookie.

A brown-and-tan puppy wiggled over to Skipper. The puppy nipped at Skipper's earphones. Maybe she wanted to hear Skipper's music! Skipper smiled. She named the puppy DJ.

The fourth puppy was scared to leave the basket. She stuck one paw out. Then

she walked over to Barbie and clung to Barbie's leg like sticky candy. Barbie named her Taffy.

The girls headed upstairs to their bedrooms. Barbie, Skipper, and Stacie remembered their rooms. They had the same beds as when they were little. They had old photos in their rooms.

There was no bed for Chelsea. There were no old photos of Chelsea either. This year, she was going to sleep in Skipper and Stacie's old room. Grandma wanted her to feel at home.

"Last time we lived here, you slept in a

crib," Skipper explained.

"There might be something of yours in the attic," Grandma said to Chelsea.

The girls followed Grandma upstairs. All four puppies followed the girls.

There were lots of things to explore in the attic. Chelsea found a cradle for the puppies.

Skipper pulled an old piece of paper out of a box. "What's this?" she asked Barbie.

"It's my treasure map," Barbie replied.

3

"Legend has it, a treasure was buried right here in Willows by the town's founders," Grandma said. She and the girls were in the kitchen, looking at the treasure map. "They wanted to make sure Willows would always prosper, and the treasure would be there in a time of need."

The puppies were nestled in their cradle. Chelsea was feeding them.

"Every summer, Grandpa and I would look for clues together," Barbie said.

Unfortunately, Barbie and Grandpa never found the treasure. Stacie, Chelsea, and Skipper wanted to look for it.

"Barbie, can you take us, *pleeeease?*" Chelsea asked.

"I'm sorry," Barbie replied. "I'm gonna hang out with Christie. Plus, my treasure-hunting days are over."

Skipper took photos of the treasure map and stored them on her tablet.

The next morning, all four girls headed into town. The older girls had bikes. Chelsea got a tricycle.

The puppies jumped into the bicycle baskets.

Barbie went to meet Christie at Willowfest. Chelsea, Skipper, and Stacie headed across the street to city hall to find the first clue. The puppies followed them.

Joe and Marty saw the girls. They also heard the girls talking about the treasure.

"Treasure?" Marty asked. "Joe, we could put air-conditioning in all the tents!"

"We could do more than that," Joe said.

Joe and Marty wanted the treasure, too. The girls went to the steps of city hall. They met Mayor Jenkins. He almost tripped on a broken step. He needed to repair lots of things in town.

"Grandma said the search begins where the town began," Skipper said. "City hall is where the town was founded."

The girls looked around. Then they saw a plaque with the Willows emblem and some writing on it.

Stacie read it aloud:

"Let the willows be your guide."

Meanwhile, Barbie found Christie in front of the Storminator ride at Willowfest.

"Barbie, it's so good to see you!" Christie said. "How long has it been? It must be long, because we were both kids—"

Barbie giggled. She forgot how fast Christie talked! The last time they had seen each other, they had been much younger. Now they wanted to relive their fun times together.

But their favorite ride, the Storminator,

was shut down for repairs! Barbie and Christie were disappointed.

"Well, I guess we can start a new tradition," Barbie said.

On the steps of city hall, Skipper, Chelsea, and Stacie were looking for more

clues. The puppies looked, too. They asked a dog named Jack for help.

"We'd like to ask you a few questions about the treasure," Rookie said. "Do you know its position?"

Jack rolled over. He tried to cover his ears. "What's a fellow got to do to get a nap around here?" Jack said. He raised his paw and touched another plaque with the Willows emblem on it. A secret panel opened in the ceiling of city hall's porch!

Stacie climbed up on a railing to read a new clue:

"We came from afar to this great land

Carrying the future in the palm of our hand."

Skipper pulled out her tablet. She found a photo of one of the founding fathers. He was holding the willow twig in a vase . . . in his hand!

"Where's that vase now?" Stacie asked.

Skipper looked at her tablet again. The vase was inside city hall!

They went inside. Then they asked the mayor to show them the vase.

Stacie shined her penlight into the vase. She saw a message on the bottom. But the letters were jumbled and unreadable.

"I think I have a mirror," Stacie said.

Chelsea looked puzzled. Why did Stacie want a mirror?

"Not for me, for the clue," Stacie said.

Stacie felt something on the bottom of the vase. She found a small willow tree charm inside a secret compartment on the vase. She put the charm on her necklace in case it came in handy later.

Meanwhile, Skipper took a picture of the message at the bottom of the vase. It was written backward.

Skipper reversed the photo image by holding it up to the mirror. Then she read the clue aloud:

"What runs for miles and never gets tired?"

"It's a riddle," Stacie said.

At Willowfest, Barbie got a text message.

"That's the girls," she told Christie. "They found another clue on their treasure hunt and are heading home." Barbie smiled. There was no harm in looking for the treasure. "Do you want to hang out again tomorrow?"

"Sorry, I've got to help my mom pack," Christie said. "At the end of the summer, we're going to live with my aunt and uncle."

Barbie couldn't believe that Christie was moving out of Willows.

"Oh, Christie, I didn't know. Is there anything I can do?"

"Oh, no thanks, Barbie. It'll be fine. Change is good, right?" Christie replied.

"Sure, yeah, right! How about an ice cream sundae? My treat!" Barbie said.

Later that evening, Barbie and her sisters ate dinner at Grandma's picnic table.

Grandma asked Barbie, "How was your day with Christie?"

Barbie was sad. Christie had to move. Her parents couldn't afford to live in Willows anymore.

"Okay, I guess," Barbie replied. "There weren't as many rides at Willowfest as I remember."

"Willowfest has gotten smaller over the years," Grandma agreed. "The mayor even thought about canceling it altogether."

After dinner, Grandma took out some old home movies to show the girls.

"Am I on there?" Chelsea asked.

"Maybe," Grandma replied. "You were a baby then."

It was true. Chelsea was a baby. Barbie, Skipper, Stacie, and Christie were in the movies, too. They were having fun at Willowfest.

Barbie thought of Christie. She didn't want her friend to move. But she wasn't sure how to help her. "I'm going to bed," she said sadly.

🐾

Joe and Marty were eating dinner on the other side of town. They were sitting outside their trailer. Marty had made corn dogs again. Joe was disgusted.

"When we get that treasure, we're going to have a feast every night," Joe said.

The girls set out bright and early the next morning.

Barbie and Taffy left first. Barbie hoped to relive some of her good memories. She even had a list of things to do. She called it her summer fun list.

She went to her old dance studio. She couldn't wait to dance there again. But Miss Melody's Dance Studio was closed!

"Oh no," Barbie said. A lot of places in town were closing.

Taffy put her paw on Barbie's list.

Barbie smiled. "You're right, Taffy," she said. "There's still more to do on my summer fun list."

Skipper, Stacie, and Chelsea also headed into town. Their puppies followed them.

They looked at the clue again:

What runs for miles and never gets tired?

"Running water!" Stacie cried.

"It's got to be Lake Willows," Skipper said.

The girls raced to Lake Willows.

Joe and Marty were working at Willowfest. They went up in a Ferris wheel. They could see the whole town. They saw the girls going to Lake Willows.

"It looks like the girls are on to another clue," Joe said. He and Marty decided to follow them.

🐾

The girls jumped into some paddle boats. Where was the next clue? They didn't see anything.

"What about the old water fountain shaped like a willow tree?" Stacie asked.

The girls quickly paddled back to shore. They ran to the fountain in the town square.

There was another plaque at the base of the fountain. It said:

Where the water flows

The willow grows.

Skipper, Stacie, and Chelsea looked up. They saw another plaque at the top of the fountain. It was too high to reach. Stacie threw a coin. It hit the Willows emblem on the plaque.

Then a door opened at the bottom of the fountain.

There was another clue inside:

Slowly progressing like a midday chime
The growth of a tree is a reflection of time.

"Time?" Chelsea said. "Look, it's the clock tower."

The clock tower was reflected in the fountain.

"The clue said 'midday chime,'" Stacie added. "It's almost noon. Let's hurry."

Joe and Marty followed them.

7

The town clock was like a music box. Little wooden animals and people popped out its front doors at noon. The clock chimed and played a song.

The girls stayed for hours. Where was the next clue for the treasure?

"Treasure hunting is hard," Chelsea said.

The girls and the puppies returned to the clock every day.

Joe and Marty returned every day, too.

They still couldn't find a clue.

Finally, Stacie figured it out. The chiming bells played a song. Skipper found the song on her tablet. Its lyrics were the next clue:

Everything you need
Lies beneath the willow tree.

"There are tons of willow trees," Chelsea said.

"But only one is the first tree!" Stacie added. The girls ran from the clock tower to the town's first willow tree. They put down their things. The puppies began to dig beneath the tree. They found coins. They found a gum wrapper. But there was no clue.

While the dogs were digging, Joe and Marty sneaked up. They took Skipper's backpack. They found the map on her tablet and other clues inside. Nobody saw them as they hurried away.

The girls and the puppies were getting tired. It was time to go home for the evening. They gathered their things.

Skipper gasped. "My backpack's gone!" Without the clues, it would be hard to find the treasure. Was it time to give up?

When they got home that evening, Skipper, Stacie, and Chelsea were tired and hungry. Barbie and Taffy were already home. Grandma fed them dinner. The puppies put their heads in the girls' laps. They nuzzled the girls to comfort them.

"The hunt is over for the summer,"

Skipper said sadly, her head in her hands.

Stacie was upset. "I'm not giving up," she said.

The puppies yipped. "We're not giving up either!" they barked.

Later, Grandma spoke with Barbie alone.

"Grandma, is the town in trouble?" Barbie asked. "Willowfest was almost canceled. Almost everything is closed or needs repairs. Christie's family is moving away."

Maybe it was time to find that treasure to help the town.

"Grandma, do you really believe there is a treasure?" Barbie asked.

"Your grandfather believed," Grandma replied. "That's good enough for me."

It was good enough for Barbie, too.

The next morning, Barbie joined her sisters for the treasure hunt. She had spent enough of her vacation remembering summers past. It was time to help Skipper, Stacie, and Chelsea.

"We don't have any of our clues," Skipper said. "They were all on my tablet."

Stacie held up the willow charm on her necklace. "Whoever took it didn't get this," she said.

"Or this," Barbie added with a smile.

She had her old treasure map in her hand.

They all looked at the song lyrics on the map. Then Barbie read the second verse aloud:

Meet me there at three

By the shady willow tree.

That was the answer! They needed to look in the willow tree's shadow.

At three o'clock, the sisters stood in the long shadow of the town's first willow tree. The sun shone off the clock tower. It cast a beam of light on the grass.

The puppies began digging right away. Soon they uncovered another plaque with a Willows emblem on it. It was all mixed up like a puzzle.

Chelsea put the puzzle pieces together. "Ta-da!" she shouted.

Then the ground began to rumble. The earth shook. Suddenly, a tunnel opened right in front of them! The girls went into

the tunnel. Soon they were in a giant cave.

Taffy whined. "It's really cavey in here,"

she whimpered.

They walked across a rickety rope bridge. It was scary.

Finally, they all reached the other side safe and sound. There was a steep cliff nearby. Barbie found an old elevator. There were ropes and pulleys. The girls got ready to move down.

"That's far enough, girls!" someone shouted. "We've got it from here."

It was Joe! Marty was with him. They had followed the clues in Skipper's backpack and were coming to claim the treasure for themselves!

"Are you guys clamped in?" Barbie whispered to her sisters.

All four girls checked their harnesses and held on to their puppies. Then they jumped off the edge of the cliff! They quickly rappelled down to the bottom of the cave.

Stacie found another plaque on the cave wall. She pressed it. The wall began to shake. Then it opened.

The girls stepped inside. The puppies

followed. Poor Taffy was too little to jump over the ledge! Barbie helped her.

"Wow!" Chelsea exclaimed. They were standing at the edge of an underground lake! They all piled onto a raft. Soon they hit some rapids.

The puppies looked on nervously. "Rocks ahead!" Taffy barked.

"We've got to navigate around this," Barbie said. The girls held on to the raft. The puppies held on to the girls! The raft bounced up and down over the whitewater currents. The raft began to fall apart!

Barbie steered the raft into calmer

waters. The girls were happy to step safely onto the shore. That was when they found the door to a giant vault. It was locked.

"How do we open it?" Chelsea asked. "Press a button? Solve a riddle?"

Barbie looked at the willow charm on Stacie's necklace. Suddenly, she got it! It

must be the key to the lock!

Within seconds, the door opened. The girls gasped. The room was filled with treasure. The puppies dove into the mounds of jewels and coins.

But then Joe and Marty caught up with the girls. They wanted the treasure.

"The treasure belongs to the city," Barbie said.

Joe and Marty ignored her. They gathered all the treasure they could. Then Joe reached for a golden plaque

set in the ground. Rocks tumbled down. Everyone ducked for cover. When the shaking stopped, they were all trapped inside the vault!

"There's got to be a way out," Barbie

said. She searched the vault for an exit.

On the other side of the wall, Taffy shook herself off. She had been separated from the others in the rock slide. She looked up and saw a giant spider. It was really scary!

"I've got to find a way to get them out," Taffy thought. She gathered her courage and jumped past the spider. She scurried up a rope ladder. Then Taffy leaped as high as she could.

Would she make it? Taffy went up and up through the air. She touched a Willows emblem. The door to the vault opened!

Light poured into the cave. Brave Taffy
trotted through an opening.

"Way to go, Taffy!" Barbie said. "She
found a way out."

Joe and Marty started grabbing more
treasure.

"The bad guys are getting away,"
Chelsea said.

"We've got to stop them," Honey barked
to the other puppies. They got ready to
pounce. The puppies circled the crooks.
They jumped up and down.

"Go away!" Joe shouted. "Shoo!" The

puppies pounced and wrapped a rope around the bad guys.

Joe and Marty fell to the ground, all

tied up. The puppies' plan had worked!

"You're not going anywhere!" Honey barked at the men.

A little while later, Grandma and Tiffany met the girls outside the cave. The police took Joe and Marty away to jail.

Grandma gave the girls a big hug.

"You never stopped believing," she said
proudly.

🐾

The next day, the mayor of Willows
thanked Barbie, Skipper, Stacie, and
Chelsea—and the puppies!

"These gals have decided to donate the
treasure to the city of Willows," the mayor

announced. "Their generous donation has saved the city!"

Christie's family stayed in town. Her father was able to get a new job. The stores reopened. The mayor had the steps to city hall repaired.

The treasure also saved Willowfest.

The girls got some of the treasure as a reward, but they had bigger plans for it. They celebrated at Willowfest. Chelsea got lots of pictures of herself.

"Next time I come to Grandma's, there will be lots of photos on the wall and lots of memories," Chelsea said.

At last, the girls had to go home. Grandma let them take the puppies.

"Mom, are you coming with us?" Taffy asked.

Tiffany nuzzled her littlest puppy. "No," she said gently. "But I'll come visit whenever Grandma Roberts can."

Later, the evening sun began to set on city hall. Barbie and Taffy finished hiding the rest of the reward treasure.

"Are you sure?" Grandma asked.

"Yes," Barbie replied. "The founders knew that the town needed to have something to believe in."

Chelsea glanced at the brand-new treasure map.

"You made sure it's hard to find?" Stacie asked.

"It will take at least a summer," Skipper replied.

The sisters smiled at one another. They couldn't wait until next year!